This book was inspired by a dog called Fred for his human sisters Alexa & Scarlet.

This book belongs to

....

Sniffy

Written by Andy & Sophie Shaw

Illustrated by Tom Pennifold

Throughout this book see if you can find Sniffy's bone hidden on each page.

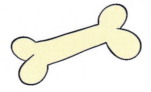

Sniffy is training to be a search dog for the Army.

For the start of Sniffy's training, he needs to learn how and where to search, for this he searches for his tennis ball. Once he gets good at this he can start searching for more important things.

His tennis ball has been hidden away

Let's see how he does on his first training day.

Sniffy's first job, is to search a sports shop.

Oh, silly Sniffy, look out for the mop!

His tail wags as he searches around

He sniffs up high and down on the ground

With a sniff and a sit and a wag of his tail

Let's see what Sniffy's found...

Oh, Sniffy!! That's not your ball, it's some old smelly socks!

Next, Sniffy searches a train track at night,

Oh careful Sniffy, look out for that light!

With an excitable bound, he searches the seats

No Sniffy, don't eat those sweets!

With a sniff and a sit and a wag of his tail

Let's see what Sniffy's found...

Oh, Sniffy!! That's not your ball, it's a slice of pizza!

His next job is to search a Royal Air Force plane,

Look out Sniffy, jump over the drain!

His nose wiggles as he runs up the stairs,

He searches the cockpit, the trolleys, and the chairs.

With a sniff and a sit and a wag of his tail

Let's see what Sniffy's found...

Oh, Sniffy!! That's not your ball, it's a pack of playing cards!

Sniffy's last job of the day is to search a superstore,

Oh no, it looks like Sniffy has hurt his paw,

With a bandaged-up leg, he hobbles on through,

Searching quite slowly, he still knows what to do.

With a sniff and a sit and a wag of his tail

Let's see what Sniffy's found...

YAY Sniffy!! He's found his tennis ball!

Good job Sniffy! Today has been a great day of training.

The Shaws

Printed in France by Amazon
Brétigny-sur-Orge, FR